AF432238

DEF - Destroying Every Fear

The Second Collection of stories

Vino Venitas

A message from Vino Venitas

Thank you for buying this book. I am currently in the process of learning how to let go of my writing. I have held these stories for myself for a very long time. Afraid that the world would look at me a certain. But now that I have grown I feel like it is time to share who I am with the world. And if you're curious as to how I grew … well reading books really helps you grow. Who knew right? I hope that at least one of these stories finds its way to helping you grow. That would be the greatest compliment I could ever receive.

Contents

1. *A mind of caution*

Another fallout, another disagreement

For their issues, there are no easements

One is open for risk, the others opt for safety

3 versus 1 each side thinks the other's crazy

They only think, then talk, then think some more

He only acts on instinct, unaware what plans are for

If you're scared to take risks, don't start a business

Planning and strategy, to be safe you need this

All you need is perseverance, motivation and a goal

If you don't know all the consequences, the end is a dark hole

Have faith in yourself, to avoid any traps

But if we get successful, there is no way back

I might lose the house, get more bills, pay extra taxes

Can't believe your mind really works like this

It's idiotic, stupid and based on fear

We haven't made a dime in the last 5 years

And yet you have the audacity to conjure up a fantasy

Where we become wealthy, in a short period of time

Is that really the best logic that you could find?

We need to read books, increase our knowledge, be patient

By the time you take action, the concept is ancient

Everything needs to be clear, every angle covered

Discuss every decision, till it's all without clutter

And so, we talk and talk about things that don't matter

How we address each other, and how things can go better

We make plans that never happen, then discuss about that

Then we discuss the corporate structure which we lack

Excuse us for trying to align 4 minds

Through dialogue we leave uncertainty behind

You also leave behind chances, money, and time

"Thanks to that we're still here," is a coward's line

…

The world is divided by a line ever true

Separating those that think and those that do

Rarely do the two exist in harmony

History has shown they'll both go crazy

Great minds think alike should be the guideline

To ensure that partners are of the same kind

Or else frustration, irritation are factors that are certain

And the parties will consider one another a burden

Which will slowly lower the business pulse

A mind of caution doesn't mix with a mind of results

Go forward or die vs we must know why

Are fuel for arguments that will not idly go by

An endless cycle in which they are caught

And some fights are just not meant to be fought

2. *Wanting to be normal*

His palms and cheek are pressed against the carton
He can hear them enjoy their plain boredom
His body shivering, he releases a sigh
His eyes show he is about to cry
He wants to go inside where it's safe and familiar
Where danger is forced to go through a filter
And time ticks to the beat that is planned out
Rain and storms are scheduled to come about
Where its cozy cause everyone knows each other
No surprises, even risk is like a brother
Unlike here where danger can go crazy
The roads are made of blades, and pitfalls are deadly
The rain is acid and the sun is dead
Being inside is the best time he ever had
The skies are grey the trees consist of fire
The wind doesn't howl, instead calls him a liar
Lured out with the promise of being unique
Never once considered himself to be weak
But the greener pastures promised turned out to be fake
A logical decision after the path he had to take
Walked here for days, months, maybe even years
All the while ignoring his talking fears
And after all that time he never reached his goal
Admitting failure will create a restless soul
It's then he gets flashes of when he was in
How he craved for more, but the walls were limiting
The corners became constraints for a mind he wished to free
The walls were closing in, it was driving him crazy
The comfort of normal, the warmth of safety

The beauty of a path walked on by many
At the time it seemed, boring, dumb and lame
Where is originality if it's all the same
His mind starts to race with the carton still touching his face
He realizes that being lucky just wasn't the case
He finally lets go and walks with his head down
Now the wind goes from liar to calling him a clown
He wonders if all the greats had to go through the same thing
And if they succeeded or heard the fat lady sing
No, they made it or else their names
would've never made it to him
He knew from the start that the chances were slim
But to do what others did is called repeating
Tired of it being their results he was seeing
For all these reasons and more he left being in
He is just exhausted of all this walking
With worn down shoes he kicks pebbles and rocks
You are looking at a mind that is tired of
thinking outside of the box

3. *He is right*

Fungus covered walls, a ceiling with a leaking pipe
An old, tattered bed on the floor, a flickering light
Tape covered windows and bugs on the floor
An old broken TV and a locked door
It's here where they talked, laughed and shared pain
It's here where they cried, and learned each other's name
Where their eyes met and silenced the screaming
Where both saw a side, neither could believe they were seeing
The reasons for it happening became irrelevant
As did the end result or the letters that were sent
In two weeks' time, they became better friends than most
Even though she was the guest and he was the host
The bruises faded away and the fear was gone
A natural development, to them it didn't seem wrong
But his partner in crime had a different mind state
But he recognized the signs a little too late
Tried to intervene but it was useless
Because both parties agreed to this
Internal struggles now somewhat of a routine
The two partners argued over what they had seen
Both felt the other's actions were unnecessary
Their discussions passed the point of being friendly
Fists were thrown and bodies were flung
As she quietly sat there holding her tongue
The plan went haywire, the situation became dire
This unexpected event can make their dreams expire
But when the word marriage was thrown, he lost his cool
As they fight, he screams "you're a goddamn fool"
Guns are drawn, he points at him, he points at her

A standoff they never expected to occur

...

Two weeks ago, they concocted a plan to get money
They would do all they can to escape poverty
Luckily, he knew a man that was stinking rich
The man had a daughter who he heard was a bitch
The plan was simple, kidnap her and get the ransom
Hold her until he pays, the payoff will be handsome
One would stay put, the other would make
sure the money is coming
But the apartment was boring, so they started talking
Talked about everything from god, to how rain falls
Then they fell in love thus ruining it all
Convinced they were soul mates, a bond without a crack
Plus, kidnapping "come on, how meet cute is that?"
The partner was enraged it was a plan with no flaw
Thus creating the whole situation we just saw

4. *I hate him*

"A hatred with no bounds, a stare that's relentless
This thing came from hell, why won't nobody notice"
…
Absolute contempt because it ruined everything
His eyes filled with disgust, it was really revolting
Agony filled his days, it was always in sight
Terror filled his dreams, it even ruined his nights
Rage filled thoughts gather for each line, each hair
Evil thoughts occurred that were never there
Drowning in the menace, his mind has become
Waking up in sweat pools, his sanity undone
Irrational and crazy that is what they now call him
Their perception is flawed, this isn't just a mere whim
Handed him more nonsense than he could count
No calculator could define the amount
Obliterate, destroy, at the very least, remove
Break the bond, and let peace once again soothe
Over and over, it seems to fail him
Underestimated this hellish thing
Never again will it catch him off guard
Deprive it of blood with a metal chord
Slice its veins with a steak knife
Actions he's been thinking of forthe latter part of his life
Sinking deeper in the depression caused by this thing
The only pure piece is the part from which it's hanging
Angry and sad, why was he given this curse
Reasoning with it only makes things worse
Every time he tries, no response is given
This piece of shit probably doesn't even listen

Happiness has been forcibly let go
And apathy grows ever so slow
Tried therapy but they just don't understand
Selfish bastards, money is all they demand
Resistance seems futile, it's like a game of chess
Endurance is key, but he just needs a rest
Longing for the day that it will be gone
Every day comes closer to it going wrong
Negativity seems to be attracted to it
Taking it, accepting it, the madness has to quit
Leave to never return
Evil creatures must burn
Senseless to stay together
Separation would be better

…

Tired of waiting, he went ahead and did it
His eyes tear with a quivering lip
Ignored the pain and the blood that came
Smiling cause, he knew this was the end game
Told them it would come, they didn't listen
Hell bent on having a life worth living
It all started when it took a letter from the mail
New reasons to stop emerged, but to no avail
Granted the fear induced adrenaline was strong
Caution should be taken in case something went wrong
After the first one, there was no turning back
Make it so, or the rest of your days will be black
Every fiber in his body fought against the anguish
For the first time since ever, he fulfilled his wish
Researched the steps a million times
Over and over he rehearsed it in his mind
Made his dream reality
Handed over his sanity
Erupted with a scream and started the process
Loved every second, the pain and the results he witnessed
Locked the doors, didn't want any interruptions

Well aware that screams like this, awake
the neighbor's conscience
Half assed efforts will not be condoned
You will not take sedatives, what's the use if you're stoned
Willpower, a knife, a towel, and something to burn
Other than that nothing is needed, it's now his turn
Now or never was the chant before he started
Try as you might, tonight you're dearly departed
Nuisance, a bother, a lifelong pest
Old grudges will now have a place to rest
Bold enough to risk my life, to take yours away
Oddest thing is I'm still waiting on what you have to say
Die, leave, burn, its time I regained my luck
Your time is finally up
Nine hacks is all it took, it was pretty easy
On this day, there is no longer a you and me
Tricked me, tricked my friends and my family
I will no longer abide by your 5-finger insanity
Controlled his own fate, finally did what he planned
Ecstasy was his, he finally cut off his own hand
…
"A hatred with no bounds, a stare that's relentless
This thing came from hell, why won't nobody notice"

5. *Evolution*

Consciousness gone, his body twitching
Teary eyed but her knuckles itching
Her fists drip blood, his eyes turned back
Where she saw red all he saw was black
Stunned by her acts all she could do was stare
This made it seem as if she didn't care
But it was for the best, she loved him more than anything
But the current situation, was simply heartbreaking
...
It started with a tap, forcing him to put it back
Discipline is the strongest without the lack of slack
Words seemed useless, one ear in, the other out
Making it look stupid to scream or shout
Time out was laughed at, gave no value to things
Taking away his stuff, became simply insulting
Then came a to do list from absurd to nasty
But then he just started planning his day accordingly
And smiled when he did them, defeating its purpose
Didn't see it as punishment more like a household service
It seemed that a tap worked best, a belt even better
Physical punishment made him listen to her
From a top to a belt, a belt to a ladle
Break his mischievous character, she just wasn't able
From a ladle to slipper, slippers to a branch
that did more than pinch
Had to switch her tool once he no longer flinched
His deeds grew in scale, trying to find his limit
Increased in danger and he seemed to love it
Took the punishment in stride and planned the next one

Uncaring what she inflicted, he saw it as fun
As the years passed, his body grew stronger
He could now take more hits, and hold out longer
Which meant she had to up her power, and number of hits
Had to bring her own hands back into this
Not old enough to drive, but more than tall enough to see
So going for a joyride became rather easy
Due to lack of experience, didn't know how to react
His first real offense just became a fact
A six-year-old hit by a car that was speeding
Hospitalized in a coma with internal bleeding
Cops brought him home, told the mother the story
Combined her discipline with her going crazy
Struck him until his screams went silent,
an inch away from death
To ensure this won't happen again as long as he draws breath
Her tears steady rolling as her mind goes back
She remembers how it all started with that small tap

6. *Leave me alone*

They gawk at me without any regard for my feelings
Amazed, baffled and shocked at what they are seeing
It could be the scars, the stitches, the bumps or hair
All invalid reasons, cause I simply don't care
Tears used to gather, my head remained down
Scared of the world, ridicule was always around
Cried myself to sleep, but even my screams were deformed
With every release police were informed
My appearance combined with the fear they hold
Gave birth to the greatest tales ever told
For mere looks make you a beast, a killer, a monster
A mindless animal with no morals or honor
Kids stay away due to the stories they've heard
This city's scarecrow, maybe boogeyman's a better word
I have eaten hearts, placed kids in my freezer
I have a supposed wide array of shining meat cleavers
I hide in closets and sleep under beds
I have jars filled with decapitated heads
When in reality, I have my bachelors, masters and PhD
The hardships to obtain those defies even insanity
The tomatoes, the stones, the words, the loneliness
My school years scars run deeper than I dare confess
But I persevered with the believe my papers would help
But with each degree, I entered a new hell
I've been denied housing, loans and even prostitutes
As a child, I was the one for whom no one roots
Chirurgy wouldn't help, I have a horrid bone structure
Repeatedly told I was nothing more than a loser
Destined to be alone, my current life proves them right

My brain is but the one tool with which I can fight
All I want is to be left alone
No peeping toms into my home
So I conjure up plans and make devices to aid me
A mind brimming with scientific ingenuity
Put to use to create a world of peace
Where mocking and laughter will finally cease
I'll make their stories reality, give them horrors unbound
I'll take away sight, sense, feeling and leave but sound
So when fear grips their hearts they can hear it pound
Simply for looks they ignored the biggest brain around
I'll subdue the world, I'll make it nice
I'm society's handmade dooms day device
They crafted my pain, created my hate
Locked away my happiness, thus sealed their own fate
I'm not a mad scientist, simply wanted to be liked
After this is over, I'll no longer have to fight
~BOOM~

7. *Passed it down*

I'm scared. Every time I hear steps in the hallway, I think it's him. My body starts to shake because it's afraid too. It's been 2 weeks since his hands balled up and hit me. They used to be open. And never crossed my face. But now his fists graze my cheek, his knuckles meet my nose. My blood decorates his shirts, which he seems to wear as a badge of honor. If I cry and cower in the fetal position, he kicks me in the stomach. Places his knee on my neck, waits till I damn near choke, then brings his fist down to my face. My tears or screams only seem to fuel his rage. He will kill me one of these days. I try to stay after school. I try to stay away. Not get into his line of sight. But he finds me, every time.

Ever since she left, his heart seeks refuge in alcohol. His mind tries to sleep in anger, he hates me. He screams it when he is on top of me, beating me till everything turns black. His tears fall on me, in between his punches. I can smell the alcohol on his breath. When he is sober, I can hear him whisper "you look just like her." Every time I pass by, I can feel his eyes burn in my back. I have no place to run, no one to defend me. I wonder when she left him if she thought of me. He used to take it out on her, I can't blame her for leaving. But for me to take her place, couldn't have been her plan, right?

I also recall the stories he told her. I placed my ear on their door to listen in. His dad often abused him. Taught him a wacked way of discipline. And showed him but one way to vent his frustration. But when I listened, I swear to god he said, "I will never hurt the two of you." This was before he got fired, before he couldn't get rehired. Before his friends didn't want to see him as much because he was bringing them down. Now his promise is nothing more than an empty shell I place my dreams in. I cover under the sheets hoping the darkness will protect me. But I can feel him pull away all that makes me feel safe. He screams things at me that are not meant for me. I'm without hope of a better future, without happiness or light. I'm lost in the abuse of my father. As a 12 year old girl, who doesn't know how to fight.

8. *Welcome back*

He listens to the seconds pass as he sits in the dark
His only interruption is the neighbor's dog's bark
Eyes closed as he relives his memories
An occasional grin for the flashes he sees
The glistening of the tools, the blood covered hands
The silence after the screams, the realization of plans
The careful strategies, the stake out, the grab
Times filled with the most fun he ever had

Each unique, each its own high
All of them had their own special way to cry
Some cussed me out, some begged for their life
Others gave me messages to give to their wives
A few remained silent, not a peep was given
Their punishment became for those of the unforgiven
The actual number I lost, but each face is clear
Those eyes drenched in immortal fear

But he gave it up, put his title to rest
A serial killer placed amongst the best
Disappeared from the public's view
A rare thing killers do
But he decided that his murder days were through
The police once again, left without a clue
Reasons for his departure doesn't matter
Combined all the resources he could gather
Bought a little house on a quiet, little street
Where him and temptations simply won't meet
And for ten long years, the voices remained silent
But then one little voice became somewhat defiant

It's whispers created paths in dreams filled with dark
Leading to a well-known and flickering mark

My eyes became sharp, my mind regained focus
Unpleasant happiness, thought I was over this
The memory flashes turned to possibilities
There is ecstasy awaiting in so many cities
New methods are devised, new alibis are created
Almost certain the old ones are too outdated
My eyes were still closed when my grin became a smile
This itch on my brain, the sensation, it's been awhile
The dog's bark has stopped, a whimper is now heard
Perhaps he sensed the switch that just occurred
Consider this the start, consider this my return
The teacher is back, there is so much more to learn
So, this letter is to notify you of the horror to come
My final streak, after this I'll be done
Make sure to print this, I want to read it in a week
This will be Vino Venitas, his best killing streak

9. *Must be a joke*

-Sleep-
His sleep peaceful, floating on a cloud of milk
His head on Egyptian cotton, his body on Persian silk
A dream amongst dreams, a rare occurrence
Softly taken away by the winds air currents
His eyelids close slowly, there's no haste to be found
A constant smirk, because there is no rage around
-Awake-
Where am I, why is everything black, I feel restricted
Why is the ceiling so close and why is it padded
Why can't I move my legs or hands, barely lift my head up
Why does it smell and taste dusty, why am I dressed up
WHAT THE FUCK is going on, this can't be happening
This is too crazy to be real, I must be dreaming
-Sleep-
A grassy field with birds chirping and a view of the sea
Rainbows, glistening water, a sight of beauty
Dolphins prance on the water, while doves dance in the sky
The suns warmth is exquisite, all of it made him cry
Pink clouds, with a gold lining, not a hint of storm around
And natures music offers the perfect background
-Awake-
Help, get me the fuck out of here
I've been placed in my greatest fear
Please open up, please get me out
Why won't someone hear me shout
It's too dark, it's too narrow, HELP ME
I'm going crazy, please HELP ME
-Sleep-

A warm summers day, and the beach on which he is sitting,
is littered with models, who look at him, flirting
With a cold glass of his favorite beverage
Here, the worries of the world have no leverage
The models are glistening, they are lotion covered
Except for a happy sigh, no words are uttered
-Awake-
I'm dehydrated how long have I been here
I'm starving, I feel that my last breath is near
Clawed my way through the cushions, the wood is too thick
Get me THE FUCK OUT OF HERE, I'm starting to feel sick
Urinated on myself, I shitted in my pants
Losing consciousness again, save me, this is your last chance
-Sleep-
…
Created a drug to help people sleep
But the rem-cycle induced was too deep
Knocked out for seven days in a dead like state
His family saw it as a scientist's fate
He tested his own drug and that's what killed him
How were they to know he was just sleeping
He will achieve the perfect dream for which he strived
Falls in and out of sleep, while being buried alive

10. Going forward

His work ethic is considered absurd
Vacation, to him is a safety word
Set goals and deadlines that have to be done
Room for failure or breaks is rare to none
Moves at top speed to match his train of thought
Till all his dreams and chances are all but caught
Moved up the ladder, climbed to the top
Stood at the zenith, forced to stop

…

I'm finally here, I really did it
The torch of victory can now be lit
All those years went and paid off
I remember my starting point at the loft
Came at 9 am, stayed till 12 am
Called me crazy, but I showed them
I'm in a penthouse office, all round view of the city
All those hours and days finally turned into money
Now I have more than I need, financially I'm in the lead
10 houses, 10 chefs and I'm the only one they feed
30 plus cars, each cost more than I dare to say
Rich and successful, oh how I waited for the day
The best people in service to take care of everything
Everything is going smoothly, no problems need solving
No advice needs to be given, it's time for me to start living
It's time to stop and smell the flowers, and
listen to the birds singing
I've made millions, can speak two languages
Play two instruments, travelled the world doing business
I've performed in front of thousands, loved with all my heart

Sky diving, bungee jumping, even build my own race kart
Made love on a beach, a plane and in the office
There isn't a field left where I would be considered a novice
I did it all, so why do I feel like I missed something
Like a sad or dangerous realization is coming
But who cares, I'll deal with it when it comes through
For now, let me set the next challenge to work towards
I have nothing more left to do … then it hit
…
The shock was immense, he had nothing left
Then the founder started a weird kind of theft
Stole from his own company, manipulated the stocks
Divided the firm and sold off the blocks
All his hard work seemed to be in vain
To the people watching he looked insane
Tried to stop him and all the jobs he was erasing
But to him his actions required no explaining
Cause going back can be seen as going forward
Depending on the direction you're facing
And insanity has a way of turning things around

11. *An Usher Song*

Fire sirens scream to move all out the way
Something is wrong, this is the fifth today
And at each scene their fear becomes twice as strong
A boom box at each one blaring that usher song
Lives have been lost and more are to come
Cause this bastard is far from done
~How it started~
An ordinary room with an ordinary man
A broken couch, a TV, and a plastic plant
Stares at the TV with a mind completely blank
His life a dead end with only himself to thank
His job meaningless, his presence barely required
Too scared to quit, too afraid to get fired
For the past ten years this has been his routine
A constant reenactment of things already seen
His hopes are gone, his dreams went to sleep
His past is dim, his future is bleak
And then it comes on, an old video clip
Too lazy to zap, so he watches it
Doesn't listen to the words but the images hold him
All of a sudden, the words return, and he hears him sing
The words grab his heart, sink into his skin
Never before has he felt such a thing
Everything is now crystal clear with his purpose found
Starts to look if the tools needed are around
Finds what he needs and immediately heads out
For 10 years he forgot what the world is about
Action, passion, life, death and fire
The latter is the one he's come to admire

~How it needs to end~
He finds an empty room, fills it with gasoline
Pushes play on the boom box and creates the final scene
He lights the matches and chants the words to the song
Sets the room ablaze, which never takes long
Steps back to watch his work, with the heat on his face
His challenge is simple, stay in the same place
The flames are beautiful but scary as well
His eyes wide open staring into the fires of hell
His fear grows too big, he gives into his dismay
Screaming like a girl, he frightfully runs away
Tries to commit suicide, but too scared to see it through
But he doesn't give up, that's not what winners do
Dozens of buildings burn, the city is covered with fear
Yet he stays motivated, with Usher singing in his ear
"I'm twisted, cause one side of me, is telling me that I need to
move on, but the other side I, wanna break down and cry."
~Gotta let it burn~

12. *Saw it Coming*

Darkness, nothingness, he found his eternal sleep
Never knew his fear of death could grow so deep
Saw it all, relived the mistakes he couldn't take back
His life flashes before him on the moment of impact
The cracks welcomed him with a hard embrace
Saw the lines get bigger at an alarming pace
And his scream still refused to come
Words left him, felt their use was done
His reflection interrupted, yet crystal clear
It's become inevitable, he has lost his fear
Sees his face in the windows, no emotion is shown
Looking up, which is down, he sees the stone
And the wind is now his only friend
Feels like forever to reach the end
It's useless there are no brakes around
His body on instinct tries to slow it down
It doesn't realize that this trip is cursed
His body tries to level out, not dive in head first
This is the first battle that he will win
Sees the faces behind the glass, shows a small grin
Like lemmings they gathered, shocked at
the proof they were seeing
When he told them their first reaction was laughing
And at times it felt like they simply didn't care
A sad lone wolf whose friends were rare
He knew the lack of it was something good
His scream didn't come, it was weird but understood
This must be the feeling of being happy
Seconds pass as a feeling covers his body

Even with the screaming wind, he can hear his heart pound
Time did not stop but felt like it slowed down
He could feel the weight on his shoulders being dropped
A final success after countless others flopped
It's finally here, the nonsense can now cease
Gravity does its work,can feel its power increase
For a few moments he feels free, like the world lost its grip
Lost everything to live for, now cashes in his final chip
That was the final step, hindsight is now too late
Arms spread wide as feet and ledge finally separate
Standing there thinking, contemplating his decision
Came here conquering doubt and mountains of hesitation
Showing a little smile, thinking he might fly
Stood there for 5 minutes, fully aware he's about to die
A slow walk to the edge even slower to get on top of it
The view of this rooftop was something he could never forget
He will not wait for help to come
Today he will jump, let it all be done

13. *Wasted Effort*

He sits in a bar <u>holding a dirty glass</u> *whispering his pain*
With his head held low <u>waiting for it to pass</u> *slowly driving him insane*
Today he lost his car <u>and confusion doesn't leave</u>
he's thinking alcohol will make it go away
Why, he doesn't know <u>answers he needs to seize</u>
but he knows it won't happen today
Weird things happen <u>lately his memory has</u>
<u>gaps</u> *afraid he is stuck in a bad streak*
And it's all handmade <u>like hole riddled maps</u> *his purpose became weak*
Recognized the work <u>it's his enemy a dark shadow</u> *he's never seen or heard*
This is not his first time <u>it refuses to go</u> *the pain it brings is absurd*
All it does is lurk <u>creating mayhem when its</u>
<u>black</u> *destroying all he's worked for*
A sick twisted mind <u>creating regret you can't</u>
<u>take back</u> *can't take it anymore*
Its origin is unknown <u>its purpose is to break me</u> *so I'll kill him before that*
But he's related to him <u>that much is easy to see</u> *a fact he can't take back*
Based on clues alone <u>he will find this man</u> *who gave him this strife*
It became a clear thing <u>saw the frame of his plan</u> *that drove away his wife*
Now answers must be given <u>and even though it's</u>
<u>scary as hell</u> *the truth must come out*
Regain the grip on reality <u>it could all end well</u> *if I remove all doubt*
But he will not be forgiven <u>if I break his face</u> *I will hear his why*
Gave into insanity <u>at a very slow pace</u> *but even with answers he must die*
There is a price to pay <u>it's a warning for all</u> *who will walk the same route*
Heard he is me, we think alike <u>the guillotine</u>
<u>won't fall</u> *if this ghost won't come out*
He must die today <u>this conspiracy must end</u> *I'll put this ghoul in the light*
It is only right <u>justice I'll defend</u> *I will not go out without a fight*

A serial killer, <u>of the circumstances he deemed</u>
<u>fit</u>, *uncaring for the lives he messed up*
Sickening to the highest degree <u>chose only the darkest</u>
<u>of profits</u> *my joy and happiness he sucked up*
A dark morbid pillar <u>in a society bending to his will</u>
<u>I am</u> *nothing but a ghost living in my own house*
My own tragedy <u>the one trying to stop the devils</u>
<u>plan</u>, *been told he comes when I have black outs*

...   .

When he's drunk his alter ego messes everything up
When he comes to everything is jacked up
Has no idea why but his answer is to drink up

My brother is a serial killer ... <u>I have discovered a</u>
<u>conspiracy</u> ... *I am living in a haunted house*

14.   *Final cut*

They visited his parents' house, his first
apartment, his current house
Then spoke with his first girl, his first wife, his current spouse
Took pictures of the houses, the schools, the family
Talked with his friends, his fans and his one enemy
Collected interviews, photo shoots, some old video clips
A stack of albums, features and of course his hits
Documented his trials, his parties and media controversy
Got the footage, the score, ready to make a movie
Arranged the scenes, the music and interview questions
Divided between his words, other people's
words, everything in sections
He directed, shot it and wrote the script
He will edit, then render his own bio flick
Took care of the outfits, the lights and of course the places
This movie will dazzle and amaze, oh the look on their faces
There were no actors, no lies, nothing more than the truth
Went into his drug abuse, and rituals before going into a booth
He went from weed to cocaine then ended up with speed
According to him that's progress, that's
growth, something we all need
Heard his own dumb remarks, his ignorance, oh he was shook
Realized his faults, his mistakes, all the wrong he's done
Looked for good people, honest friends, but he had none
His circle was barren, empty, absolutely desolate
Yet it was filled with liars, drug dealers,
and men with yes on their lip
But this movie was raw, it was real, everything was true
Called him a junkie, an addict told him we're worried about you

Too high, too self-absorbed to listen to it the first time
Heard it too often, too many times to pay it any mind
The final cut was done, it was finished, it never got released
He was too ashamed, too embarrassed but his behavior ceased
He doesn't shoot, he doesn't smoke, drinking got stopped too
Its cause he's dead, he overdosed, so it's kind of hard to
A final hit before he quit, felt like he needed it
Since it was his last, he wanted a blast, guess he overdid it

15.   *I'll create what I want*

Damn … I don't know if the value will drop or increase

Well at least my mind can find peace

I mean it didn't really bother me as much when I bought it

But after a while I just felt the hatred

The money I laid down just to get this place

Just to have a building's wall in my face

At first it was charming, they were known worldwide

But after the first year that logic simply died

I wanted them gone but not like this

This wasn't part of my wish

I wanted it out of sight, not drop the whole thing

What I wanted to do was bad, but this is horrifying

The smoke, the fire, their screams of death

The sight of their pain, takes away my breath

My tears won't stop, I'll never forget this day

But for some reason this stupid grin just won't go away

In this world of hurt and sadness, my small care is happy

The sight I'm beholding is far from crappy

No, it's terrible, it is, those at fault must pay

But for some reason, I have never seen a brighter day

Always knew this day would come, but like this, it feels wrong

But what is done is done, I've waited for so long

No, look at the dust, the blood, the debris

And how that river now looks like the sea

It's beautiful, no no, it's crazy

Ah heck, I know it's bad but I am happy

I placed a few strategic bombs, to scare everyone

It would have burned down one floor,
would've been a job well done

But to drop the whole building is just insane

This will be the world's pain and a nation's shame

An attack of this level is considered movie stuff

I should look away, my eyes have seen enough

I will have nightmares for years, I'm sure of it

Today's actions are vile but the results, terrific

Saw my bombs go off, they combined with the other attack

You can say they punched the head while I ruptured its back

And thanks to them, my crime became mass homicide

But thanks to them, the notion of me being caught died

I love and hate what happened today

It's terrible to be happy about this, but hey what can I say

I'm sure the city will go into a horrible state

But that is their problem, with those damn twin towers gone

My window view of the city is great

16. *They woke us up*

Big metal doors open shining light on the two
Still fast asleep cause this is all they do
The rattling of their bed takes them from their dream
As they are headed for what they think is routine
Fat Man: What is it now, can't they see I'm sleeping
Little Boy: This is the only fun we have, please stop complaining
Fat Man: I'm not complaining, all I'm saying is do it at a later time
Little Boy: The early bird catches the worm, so I don't mind
Fat Man: Would you cut it out, it's too early for that stuff
Little Boy: For motivating yourself, it's never early enough
Fat Man: Yeah, Yeah, so how long do you think today will be
Little Boy: No idea but flying feels lovely
Fat Man: It doesn't bother you we're going
to live forever in the dark
Little Boy: Not really, cause our death will leave a terrible mark
As they go outside their bodies are met with rain
Then they slowly board a nameless plane
Their straps are placed on, there are less than usual
The measures for safety, this time seem rather dull
Fat Man: Oy, is it just me, or do you feel a bit more freedom
Little Boy: No, no, it feels like these chains can be easily undone
Fat Man: You don't think …
Little Boy: No, it doesn't feel like the brink of insanity
Fat Man: Don't forget we are talking about humanity
The plane takes off and takes the two into the air
And for more time than they are used to, they are kept there
Fat Man: What is going on, the training ground is close by
Little Boy: Maybe they want to see for how long this plane can fly
Fat Man: I've got a bad feeling, something doesn't feel right

Little Boy: Would you stop worrying and just enjoy the flight
Little Boy: There is simply no way they will put us to use
Fat Man: I really hope that is the truth
Their discussion interrupted as four men came marching in
They take the chains off the two while nervously shaking
Not a word was spoken, they left once they were done
Little Boy: I know what you want to say but don't jump the gun
Fat Man:...
The hatch beneath them opens up, the tension intensifies
Little Boy: Now you will see we're still over desert skies
Now the hatch is fully open, they see a sight they've never seen
A city filled with people right below this deadly team
The two remain silent, staring at the scenery
Little Boy: Humanity is doomed
Fat Man: I totally agree
Their final chains are released as they fall to the earth
On impact, a mushroom cloud is given birth
Two nuclear bombs dropped on Hiroshima, Japan
Little Boy and Fat Man became symbols for the nature of man

17. A search for Purity Part 1

+ The Year Is 1229 +

An eerie wind blows through the empty streets
Silence covers the town but the tension speaks
Their response would make you think we came to pillage
But our arrival is meant to save the village
Our actions are justified by the almighty himself
We ensure they remain blessed by god's bountiful wealth
Whispers of non-believers reached the church's ears
We were sent to abolish all of society's fears
There will be a fair trial once the culprit is found
They are here, the stench of a false deity is around
I can feel my hands itch, it's been too long
Let's find these abominations, the hunt is on

...

This village resided in a terrible state
They actually had a church where they would congregate
And worship this false god, this deceiver of men
There are bound to be more, but for now we found ten
Held a trial and they pleaded guilty
Openly admitted to worshipping another deity
They refused to listen to logic or reason
There is but one god, to believe otherwise is treason
Left us no choice but to show them the light
We deprived them of food for 6 days and 6 nights
They wouldn't confess to sin, so the next step had to begin
Fresh burning coals were placed against their skin
The smell of charring flesh is an acquired taste
As are their screams when the stones are placed
I hope they understand we're not here to hurt anybody

We want a confession and a return to Christianity
But these ten hold strong, their delusions are extreme
They hold a strong willpower, rarely seen
So now the 'we' turns to 'I', it's my turn
Not here to torture, but to help them learn
The price of abandoning god is a steep one
But they will be true believers when I am done
Hang them by their arms, place a ball and chain at their feet
Pull the rope by which they hang, till their body starts to speak
The sound of their arms out the sockets,
their vertebra starting to crack
It is at that point I release a spiked chain on their back
After 5 lashes I place a small incision in their side
Make it bigger with my finger, then slowly let it go inside
It's all to make them understand that they need to return
I'm hurting their body now, so their soul won't burn
A confession was given after their hands went missing
Now I'll visit a fellow inquisitor for my own saving
We can release each other's sins, turn our souls back to pure
So we can enter heaven's gates, we are the non-believers cure
I stand proud as I listen to one of my reborn Christians happy sobs
I helped him come back to god … man I love my job

18. A search for Purity Part 2

+ The Year Is 2020 +
This is not the work of a man but that of a group
The proof of how low madness can stoop
And each murder scene has been given a title
In blood they write a verse from the bible

…
Leviticus 26:27-30
With a smile on his face, "here is what we'll do"
I'll take care of the parents, I'll leave the kids to you
They will starve for six days, and six nights, they'll be ready
Their penance for being godless will be heavy
Burn down the house and everything they own
Let the fear of god's power seep into their bones
The kid's flesh will be cut and presented to the starving two
They will be told to eat their children's flesh,
if you want god to forgive you
Our god is jealous, and he knows no mercy
Your god is a fantasy, we'll bring you back to reality

…
Numbers 25:3-4
This group has the nerve to work on god's day
They see god's miracles but choose to look away
These are atheists who refuse to pray
For all their years of neglect, they will finally pay
We're merely here to collect, let god have mercy on their soul
We will sever their heads and place them on wooden poles
Facing a brick wall to never see a sunrise
Our actions are true in a world filled with lies
For the rest of eternity, they can look away

Neglecting god is now a dangerous game to play
…
Exodus 12:29-30
They surrounded the city, an army extremely organized
Las Vegas, a place god always despised
They believe this miracle will make the world go berserk
At the strike of 12 am, they march in to do gods work
Break into clubs, stores, restaurants and houses
Guns drawn, this job requires some swiftness
They start shooting and killing anyone they deem fit
Child, woman or man, god's wrath, they are it
Las Vegas is overcome by a gun-made storm
Tonight, they will kill all first born
…
1 Samuel 15:2-3
A peaceful village but god is not their deity
This gave birth to god's vengeful jealousy
The same army, with the same motive, forced their way in
But now everyone was deemed fit for erasing
They killed man, woman, infant, suckling and sheep
The entire village was put to sleep
After the deed was done torches were thrown
They burned down everyone's home
Human, cattle, pets, all of their lives were gone
Never was the power of god so strong
…
The authorities caught a few, but their leader is still free
And it seems more people are joining the insanity
The news received an envelope, the front said "from god's son"
The letter inside was a hint of what's to come
Isaiah 13:15-16

19.   3rd Degree Warfare

Their shields are up, blocking everything inorganic and organic
Their space time radar confirms there's no need to panic
The captain of the ship just subdued a riot
Rations are low, a force fed diet
Hunger, rage, mutiny, feeling home sick
Became the underlying theme for this trip
They have been shot at by trigger happy Shi'lans
Chased by blood thirsty Riv'ans
Escaped death by inches and extinction with mere luck
Exhausted half their fuel, and in more than one gravitational pull,
got stuck
They push forward, they have a job to do
Sleep with one eye open, and that's for their own crew
Some have more than others, which is cause for jealousy
Unwillingness to share, gave birth to a streak of robberies
Occasionally landing to restock what was lost along the way
With each time, their problems just seem to melt away
But with time they all return more vicious than before
With the current state of crew and ship, survival isn't guaranteed
anymore
The captain's speeches seem to decrease in power and feeling
The morals holding back chaos are slowly fading
The pilot to relieve stress started sleeping with the captain's wife
The guards are tired of no food, yet having to risk their life
It's rumored the captain is getting high, but he denies it
A well-known fact that the vice-captain is a raging alcoholic
The chief of security is considered to be obscene
Got caught jacking off to the men's shower camera screen
The fighter pilots lost all the team spirit and trust they had

All thanks to one big poker game gone bad
The head of technology is distracted, his wife is expecting
She is 3 months along, problem is for 6 months they haven't been sexing
And then there's the hero, the ships backbone
He sneaks into the cafeteria and devours food all alone
Their goals need to be achieved rather sooner than later
Before the crew becomes its own annihilator
Their mission is simple, they have to find an alien race
Befriend them and make them come back to their place
But they get refused on every planet on which they stop
It's becoming painfully clear, this mission is a flop
But that is a thought the captain will never confess
Can't return without at least one success
The problem is the news about humanity travelled through the galaxy
Their hunger for conflict and war has become legendary
Even this ship called Unity, showed humans at their best
Human nature always fails peace, when put to the test
So, it scours the universe, this one lonely ship
In search of anyone they can be friends with

20. *So this is it?*

Feels like I'm caught in the sickest game a mind can play
These four walls seem to be closing in every day
Keep losing track of time, every day is the same
This routine of captivity will drive me insane
Three meals a day and from time to time, it gets cleaned
Shit in the room where I sleep, starting to feel like a fiend
It's disgusting, no one should have to live like this
Could name a million things, but its freedom I mostly miss
Freedom to choose my food, freedom to see new things
Freedom to experience adventures and see what life brings
Instead, I bang my head against a wall that won't move
Life lost all meaning, I have nothing more to prove
My tears disappear in the pain in which I swim
I can feel it's my mind I'm slowly losing
My guard looks at me, with a face as if we're cool
It's proof of the fact that he takes me for a fool
I remember the past, my mind and body were free
Everyday peaceful, yes, I was truly happy
Girlfriends by the dozens, each one a beauty
Refused to be tied down, there were a lot of fish in the sea
But look at me now, sad and all alone
With four walls and a shitty looking bed to call my own
Captured, kidnapped, incarcerated, whatever the term
I'm here against my will, patiently waiting for my turn
To receive deaths touch, or maybe I should just give it up
And end it myself, I've clearly run out of luck
I'm in a manmade hell called solitary confinement
My guard is too dumb to notice when I'm being defiant
I feel like I'm going around in circles and truthfully, I am

But that is what he wants, that is his plan
To see me breaking down, to see me lose it
Until that day, his torture won't quit
He won't let me go, no matter how I beg or plea
I'm certain that he is out to kill me
But I'll return to where I'm from, if it's the last thing I do
You hear me, you bastard, if need be, I will kill you
…
No one can hear him talk, his screams are in vain
He is right, the guard simply doesn't see his pain
But the guard loves him that much is a fact
And if it's up to him, he will never send him back
But true common ground between the two will always stay blank
Because the guard is an owner of a fish in a fish tank

21. *Smiling tears*

Past: The door slowly creaked open, allowing the light to creep in

Present: Eyes wide open, yet it feels like he's dreaming

Future: His tears won't stop flowing, his mind won't stay quiet

Past: Knows what's coming but tries to ignore it

Present: A tattered grin slowly forces its way in

Future: His body screams in pain can't believe what's happening

Past: His fists are clenched knows this won't go away

Present: Thought it impossible yet prayed for this day

Future: Will never get used to this sensation of disgust and pain

Past: Remains silent for he knows screams are in vain

Present: The words he heard, made him happy, a rare thing to feel

Future: Tells himself it's a nightmare, it isn't real

Past: His eyes closed, clearly hears his footsteps

Present: Thinking "this is what that bastard gets"

Future: He will awake to see this was all an illusion

Past: This will be another horrid intrusion

Present: His life is his to do with what he will

Future: A tear drops from his closed eyes as he lays perfectly still

Past: With each time he dies, his soul is all but gone

Present: His heart smiles but his logic tells him it's wrong

Future: This defies common sense, his luck should not be this bad

Past: Security is past tense, if it was ever to be had

Present: The answer dances in his head, his eyes have lit up

Future: Between comfort and hell, once again he's stuck

Past: His body feels heavy, his breath, liquor free

Present: There's only one correct route and it's a beauty

Future: His body feels heavy, the smell of alcohol is clear

Past: Thanks to his actions the whole world I fear

Present: Death shouldn't come swift, to those of his kind
Future: Once again happiness is left behind
Past: My body shakes as it starts bleeding
Present: For once I will have the taste of peaceful sleeping
Future: My dreams are shattered, my will is broken
Past: The gifts are nothing but an empty token
Present: I'll repay it all with a high interest rate
Future: The future means nothing if this is my fate
Past: People take my silence as me being weird
Present: His eyes show it will be exactly what he feared
Future: Maybe it's my fault, maybe I am to blame
Past: My world is filled with nothing but pain
Present: His world is filled with nothing but pain
Future: This world is filled with nothing but pain
Past: Every Friday night is a night where he shivers
Present: His father will die unless he gives him his liver
Future: Placed in a foster home that seemed really endearing
Past: Every week his own father molested him
Present: He won't give it, he died, easiest decision he ever had
Future: History repeated, molested by his foster dad

22. Say it ain't so

Today is the day, the moment of truth is near
Their wedding day is finally here
They are going to seal a love so true
Keeps pacing back and forth repeating, "I do, I do, I do"
His entire family and all his friends are present
But her family decided to remain absent
Her cousin withheld the reason, but gave a hint as to why
"It's not our place to say, but we can't stand behind a lie"
He wonders of course what the secret may be
But we all have secrets and she makes him happy
She knows exactly how he wants to be treated
Arguments between the two never get too heated
Knows all his spots, knows exactly what to do
Damn near perfect, almost too good to be true
She can't bear children, but hey they'll adopt
Every time he sees her, the world seems to stop
Everything she does makes him feel better as a man
That's why he stayed, where in other
relationships he would've ran
Their first kiss was romantic, their first time was insane
Climaxed over and over, till friction turned to pain
She did what he wanted, she gave what he craved
Went from being dominant to being a slave
And now the tux is on and the dress is white
Reserved the most expensive suite for tonight
There is a swan of ice, the catering is sublime
The event seems to roll smooth, everything is on time
The bride's maids look hideous, the bride looks perfect
It's been rehearsed and practiced, no turning back

Butterflies in his stomach for the step he's about to take
Cause his vows will be the biggest promise he will ever make
But her pace is different, her face looks pale
Cause a marriage based on a lie is bound to fail
Walks back and forth, pondering to confess or not
To reveal this secret will take all that she's got
This will be the last chance for her guilt to cease
If it's not now, she will forever hold her peace
She walks to his room and knocks 3 times
She decided to get this off her mind
He told her its bad luck, she said it's bigger than that
5 minutes before their wedding, the two quietly sat
She started with, "I can't believe we are here"
"Your love and trust is what I hold dear"
"So I have to be honest, before we go on"
"My family isn't here, cause they think it's wrong"
"For me to not tell you who I was or who I am"
"Let me just flat out say it: I was born a man!"

23. *Crazy Bitch*

Another email I will not be opening
What the hell is she smoking
Calls me in the middle of the night to tell me her day
This bitch doesn't listen to a word I say
Tell her to leave me alone, and get gone
She tells me that, that would be wrong
Hacked my email accounts, she even tapped my phone
She breaks in and leaves some of her stuff at my home
Called my mom and went by for dinner
My mom then told me that she is a winner
Crazy bitch

I know he loves me, just afraid to say it
Deep down he doesn't want me to quit
It's only natural you fight to make things better
Just like our songs says, "we belong together"
My actions might seem a bit weird to some
But I'll be on top when it's said and done
Eventually he will see what he means to me
And that by my side is where he needs to be
There is a thin line between love and hate
Our love is bound by fate
My man

How sweet of her to come visit
She said she loved my boy and meant it
Saw his baby pictures and damn near cried
This is one girl he doesn't have to hide
Sweet, smart and a looker too
Hold on to this one is what he should do

Asked if I had a spare key to his place
She lost hers, so I gave it, she had an honest face
She calls me weekly to see how I've been
Hope he knows how to keep such a sweet thing
My boy and his lovely girl

Hope she takes her meds, or else it could go real bad
I don't ever want a repeat of the situation we had
She missed our appointments, doesn't answer her phone
I even sent my assistant to her home
Where could she be, I hope she didn't fall in love
And if she did, I hope she doesn't bring out the glove
And please don't let him bring the police into it
Please don't be love, please don't let that be it
The pharmacy said she hasn't come for a refill
I know it's idle, but I hope her voices remain still
My patient

I don't see it, looks like quite the catch
A pretty face and a body to match
I could get it if she was hideous or obesity type fat
But who would get a restraining order against that
Staring at us, must be afraid to come closer
I don't get it, this guy really looks like a loser
She deserves better, he deserves a lot less
Maybe I'll ask her out, when this is put to rest
There is no way this chick can be that wrong
That outfit is bad, but what's with the glove she has on
The start of a crime scene

24. *Smiling between the lines*

S – S – Sn – Sn – Sni – Sni – Snif – Snif – Sniff – Sniff

So, me and my friend Bob went to the club, right. We left around 10 cause if you get in before 11, it's free. We didn't want to waste any money on the door, we had like enough money for 2 drinks, and we didn't want to waste one on the door. I mean how sad would it look if 2 guys shared the same drink. If it was a quick sip it would be alright, but like I said, 2 drinks, so these motherfuckers had to last all night. So, we couldn't do it, we couldn't do it. We didn't wanna share. So, we sat there and waited till the club got full. And man did it get full. So, we stood there looking at girls. You know how you stand there looking to see if someone is looking at you, so you can get your flirt on. Cause only psychopaths approach women cold turkey. So, while I'm standing there scouting, this big girl gets in front of me and starts grinding on me.

Now, have you ever been so surprised, you just stood there and let it happen to you, while you are trying to figure out what the hell is going on? So, I couldn't move, but I was still looking around, but this time it was to make sure no one was looking. Cause this could hurt my chances. Now, don't get me wrong, I don't have a problem with big girls. But it just wasn't that time, fellas you know what I mean. After having sex with a bunch of skinny girls you want to mix it up with a big girl. No, no? OK, maybe that's just me. But either way, it wasn't that time, I was looking for a slim chick. But ok, so after big girl was done with me, she turned around said thank you and walked off, like nothing happened. Didn't buy me a drink, nothing. I felt used. I'm not gonna lie to you, I felt used. So, I do my final check up to make sure nobody saw, and I see Bob looking at me, holding our drink, shaking his head.

Yeah, it's our drink, we miscalculated, we only had enough for one, but who cares right? So, he's looking at me, with this look like, "dude, that's wrong." So, I gave him a look back like, "dude, what was I to do?" So, he looks back with a, "tell that bitch to move" look. So, we started this whole conversation with nothing but looks, and people noticed it, and started joining in right. So next thing you know, the whole club is making faces thinking this shit is a dance. And I swear to God that was how krumping started. No bullshit, no jokes that was the beginning of that stuff. I mean you see their faces, they must be trying to tell you something.

So, after the dance shit was through, the whole club looked at us, like we did something amazing. We felt good, cause the chances of us getting some tonight, just went through the roof. And wouldn't you know it, I still left with the fat girl that was grinding on me. But it's aight though, I did better than Bob, he left the club alone, looking at me like "dude, that's wrong." But it's aight though, I had a good time with big girl, I'm not sure if I fucked her fat or her P..., but it was good, yes indeed it was good.

...
Comes off stage with his lines ready
Grabs a straw and proceeds to stay happy
The fuel behind this comedic clown
Puts it up his nose and bends down

S – S – Sn – Sn – Sni – Sni – Snif – Snif – Sniff – Sniff

25.   *So I laugh*

As I fell off my bike and scraped my knee

He told me stop crying, I looked like a sissy

The emotions got too strong

I cried during a movie, got told it looked wrong

When I hit my head on a wall

I was told to suck it up before I could let a tear fall

Our house got robbed, took everything we owned

She told me, don't cry, no matter the issue

Not even sniffling I'm allowed to do

My girl said it was weird, but she didn't care

I loved her, she was always there

No matter the trial or the degree of adversity

Until the moment the world crumbled around me

I walked in on her fucking another bloke

And even though my heart literally broke

And I was dying inside, and the pain wouldn't stop

Not a single tear was dropped

Instead, I …

When I was down, life gave me another kick

My mother became extremely sick

It was cancer, the terminal kind

Once again, I left all joy behind

Sat by her bed, watched her veins turn black

Saw the tears fall from her eyes, I'll never forget that

She bit her lip to keep down the screams of pain

My inability to help, drove me insane

All I could do was sit and watch her die

And even then, I was unable to cry

Instead, I … like it …

At her burial it was raining, and I hoped the clouds never cleared

It felt good to pretend that the rain were my tears

When her casket dropped, I looked at the sky

My life was barren, felt like I should die

My body was shaking, my lip was quivering

Everything I loved was gone, and still I wasn't crying

People stared at me, no one seemed to get it

Even with all their looks I couldn't quit

The pain ran too deep, the scars were too long

Life had won, the agony was too strong

I had no words, but I had to vent

I had to release the anguish of my heart's dent

This is my version of letting it all go

This will allow me to heal no matter how slow

My girl is a slut, my mother is dead

Usually, you cry to let people know you're sad

Instead, I laugh like it doesn't matter

26. *Good V.S. Bad*

Prologue

The year is 3001

By 4 epidemics that spread worldwide

No soul was spared, logic left defied

2 diseases became dominant, the standard for good

Their symptoms were minimal, their consequences understood

The other 2 considered bad, their symptoms vividly clear

Their appearance and behavior made it seem more severe

The human race got divided between vampires and zombies

This is the tale of their struggle for global supremacy

~...~

Vampires

Vampires might seem calm at first, but once overcome by thirst, their face starts to twitch, and their body starts to hurt. Their eyes will lower slowly, and their temper will grow. For without the taste of fresh liquid, their beast comes out. Their senses become dull, and their inner ghoul comes out. The second degree of vampire is somewhat obsessed with fire. They blow out ecstasy as they dine on their prey, their symptoms become severe if they don't dine for one day. But due to a constant supply, their productivity never dies. Their world is that of working and ignoring their disease. The vampires occupied all the major cities.

~...~

Zombies

Zombies function on escaping pain they once felt, constantly complaining about the cards they were dealt. Their clothes are rags, dirty and old, their lack of awareness makes them bold. Constantly searching for funds not their own, cause every cent they have goes to their disease gone wrong. Their smell disgusting, their acts obscene, truly the lowest form humanity has seen. The second degree of zombies never has a straight walk, it slurs its words when it tries to talk. The reason is because it's brain is dead, so it's logic will always be nothing else but bad. It's vision is blurry, it's coordination is messed up, it's aggressive but honest. In the slums of society is where they are stuck.

~...~

Epilogue

The two battle almost every day. Because the viruses didn't discriminate. So, families were ripped apart, all due to symptoms given by a man-made disease. Brothers argue with mothers about their affiliation with a group. Sisters beg fathers to leave and become part of a select few. For the last few decades these monsters went head-to-head. Good versus Bad, but all monsters, nonetheless. But now there are a few who have cleared themselves of any disease. But their words land on deaf ears, for normal is to be afflicted with a disease.

Zombie 1st degree: Hard drugs user / Addict / Junkie

Zombie 2nd degree: Alcohol Drinkers / Addict / Alcoholic

Vampire 1st degree: Coffee drinkers / Addict / Coffeeholic

Vampire 2nd degree: Smokers / Addict / Junkie

27. *Winning is everything*

Ok, so I wake up, stretch, and get out on the right side of the bed
I shake my head twice then place my left hand on my head
Then stretch again and take exactly 15 steps to the bathroom
I sit down and start singing B.E.P.S boom, boom, boom
I finish up then make me a 6-eggs cheese omelet
4 toasts, 2 juices and my breakfast is set
I eat while watching my highlights DVD
With every touchdown, I have to yell, look that's me
Then I take a shower after I look at the time
And in the shower, I sing temptations cloud nine
Dry my body with the red towel, do my face with white
Take a look in the mirror, tell myself that's right
Put on my game day jockey and the rest of the outfit
Take a final look in the mirror and tell myself this is it
Take the elevator to the garage, circle the car one time
Get in, start it, then wait for pac to say my line
"I won't deny it, I'm a straight rider, you
don't wanna fuck with me"
Then I pull up, drive off nice and easy
The route is set, a detour must NOT come up
And if I don't speed past one red light, it's all messed up
The CD playing is set, I cannot skip one song
The absolute necessary words, I rap along
I arrive and park headfirst into my space
Then I calmly place my hand in front of my face
Close my eyes and scream all the tension away
Then skip the CD to Jay's, what more can I say
Wait till it's done get out and run to the door
Then for the first 10 steps I only watch the floor

Then I greet my teammates even the unimportant ones
And then the most important part comes
My handshake with the coach and his nod of fire
After which I suit up and scream, "well trained fighter"
Then I slap my helmet twice, and jump up and down
For about 10 seconds and then I look around
And watch these superstitious idiots with
their dirty socks and shirts
Their belief in dirt is so dumb it hurts
Then the coach gives his speech and we give a final shout
We bump helmets and chests and then we head out
And before I go onto the field, I take a final look up
Whisper to myself, "skill has nothing to do with luck"
I told you everything that I do
You must have found a clue
Tell me doc, what did I miss, what did I do wrong?
I missed my first catch in 12 years, my confidence is gone
My pre-game ritual is missing something, go on fill me in
I need to add something, don't I, or else I won't win
The psychiatrist looks at him with a blank stare
He wants to help him, but the words just aren't there

28.　　　26 Times

An anti-social, avid adversary against anything abiding an age accustomed and amped and accepting atrocious art, arenas are ancient.

Buildings built by blind business best believe, before blowing becomes basic blocks blocking bad blood, banks been broken.

Crime carelessly carries chains creating cold, calculating, critters calmly, counting chances, craving consumption, circuses circulate cancer.

Dreams defy deeds done dastardly, dreading dark dogs digging, discovering, drowning darkness deals death daily, Disney disappears.

Elegantly erasing every enemy eager enough, eradicating enigmas easily, entering enlightenment, earnestly ending embedded evil, Exxon establishments evaporate.

Finally freeing false franchises from falling further, finding fleeting fantasies fake, fostering foes forgotten, factories finally finished.

Giving great gestures, gruesome grooming, gathering gross gaining's generating greed gone global, Game 'R' Us guaranteed gone.

Hands hail hatred, hoping help has had his hiatus, heading home held horrendous heads high, history hides hell. Hospitals have holes.

Intently irritating intelligence, ideas immobilizing imagination, introduces images into infants, inspiring infernos, Ikea is incinerated.

Jaded jokes jam jaws, jobs just jittering jazz, journals join jewels, jealous junk, jumping justice, Jesus, jails jacked.

Kind killers kiss kings, kindred kids keep kicking kin, kept knowledge, knives kneeling knees, Krispy Kream killed.

Longing longer lives, lucid lies leave love, learning lessons left lonely, looks lost like lions licking leopards, ludicrous limits, let Lego lose limbs.

Magic makes minds mild, malfunctioning millions, mold my morbid mist, motivating me more, merciless, McDonalds must mend.

Negating never needed new nails, naming nice noise notes negative, nastiness nesting near numbers, Nike notices nothing now.

Opening old only offers, obstacles, opportunities oozing obvious obligations, odd ornaments over odes omitted, occurring operas obliterated.

Preaching pollution, perpetrating peace, passing past painful pillars placed precisely, pestilence personified, psychiatrists' places perished.

Qualifying quantity, questioning quests, quenching, quitters quite quietly, quizzing quality quarterly, quickly queuing quicksilver.

Rude replies receive regret, risking rampaging rage, racing rivals reach roads rarely remembered, rest, restaurants receive ridiculous retribution.

Stupid servants see similar stones sinking slowly, so savage souls stroll, seeking salvation, supermarkets shall sight shocks supreme.

Taking time twisting thoughts, troubling tales told to those treading through terrible terrain, trains took true tribulations.

Ushering unique ultimatums, uttering used, unusual, ugly undertakings, unconventional, unarmed Utopias understand unhappiness, Universities unmasked.

Vile vigilance, vacates vermin, vomiting vague vaccinations, valuing versatility, venturing very viable ventures, Volvos views violated.

Who, what, where, when will weather wrong winds, waiting whether worship wont worsen with weakness, windmills will wade within wisdom.

X chromosoming, Xanthippes Xeroxing Xmas, Xing Xrated XXX, xenophobic Xfiles, Xtra, X-axis, Xmarks Xplode.
You yank yards yapping, yelling yes, yet yesterday, young yuppies yielded youth, yachts y'all yoke yellow
Zions zealous zenith zigzagged zeitgeists zapping zeus, zombies ziplocked, zoned, zoo's zilch zero.
…
Panic gripped the world, as everywhere a letter was received. Stating only 2 lines, yet their meaning was clear. He travelled the world blowing up locations, buildings, and everything else stated in his letters. He started with A to end with Z, they dubbed him the alphabet bomber.

29. *Can't help myself*

Hook
How would it feel, if the world had just stopped?
What would I see if I couldn't feel a thing?
Would I be gone, or could it be wrong
To not want to be here?
But I'm so tired of not having any hope
All I see, is a life of empty
~
So, tell me, why oh why should I try to smile
When inside I'm slowly dying
My tears won't show, but I need you to know
That I need to let it all go
I want to hurt myself just to see if I'm still alive
But I'm afraid of losing only a part of me … so tell me
~Hook~
I pretend to be happy for the sake of my friends
I pretend to be smiling for the sake of my family
But the mash is slowly fading away
And I'm afraid to show you the true me
Want to hurt the world for making me like this
Peace of mind has become my darkest wish
~Bridge~
Jump off a bridge, cut my wrist
Stand on the highway till a speeding car hits
Jump off a building, drug myself to sleep
Or just get a gun and let my mind hit the street
So please tell me
~Hook~
I don't want to do this no more, no more

I'm so tired
I just want to be free, please let me be
The world is a dark and lonely place
Please let me go, let me be
~Hook~

30. Suit, Tie, Watch and Phone

They sit at her desk, casually drinking coffee
He tells her he has yet to receive his money
She is shocked and does a quick check up
Your name isn't in the database, "always my luck"
This has happened before, she said she would fix it
Shakes her hand saying please don't forget
Goes back to his office and starts typing away
He seems frustrated every single day
But when behind his desk a smile won't leave his face
That let his fellow workers know he loves this place
Started last month been here every day since
He is slowly becoming the office's prince
Always willing to listen, helps whenever he can
Carries boxes, gives advice, such a charming man
But when it comes to work, he does not play
He is always the very last one to stay
To his coworkers, his work drive just won't quit
Typing behind his desk, often fell asleep behind it
He is here more than he is home, it's sad yet inspiring
And he sure does love the company's free catering
Always here before everyone else, you'd think he stayed the night
Yes, he's the office's hard working, charming knight
Dressed in a black suit, red tie and iPhone
The way business should look when it leaves home
The screen is cracked but he won't send it back
He says repairing it means mobile downtime, he can't afford that
No one really remembers hiring him
Yet they all agree it's a good thing
No one has seen his work, but they assume it's great

How could it not be, he worked on it till late
When they go for business trips, they buy him drinks and dinner
He always thoroughly thanks them, the guy's such a winner
No one noticed he's worn the same suit for a month straight
And there is a valid reason why he is never late
He has secrets he doesn't want anyone to know
This is a chance he must not blow
He just walked in, started working, no one said a thing
They just assumed he was the new guy they were hiring
The amount of typing is indeed absurd
But he doesn't type sentences, sometimes not even words
He found the iPhone as well as the suit and tie
He looked too good to not give a new scheme a try
With confidence he walked in and did what others do
A place to sleep, free food, yes, a dream come true
When his coworkers find out, they might be pissed
There is a homeless person living in their midst
Something that would usually never fly
Let's call this the power of a suit and tie

31. Heavenly Trilogy: Lost in translation

Every system will make a mistake
Even perfection will eventually break

~ ~ ~ ~ ~

His eyes remain closed, fear gripped them tight
Preparing himself for the worst of sights
His body shakes, he's drenched in sweat
His muscles tense, his mind is set
His skin feels warm, as if touched by the sun
Keeps up the tension, pain is about to come
He doesn't smell sulfur, nor does he hear screams
Slowly opens his eyes to a beautiful dream

~ ~

Yet to realize what has been done
Unaware of problems yet to come

~ ~

Grazes the clouds, gazes at the blue sky
Overwhelmed by the view, he starts to cry
Falls to his knees, his head is lowered
Has so many questions, but not a word is uttered
A smile appears, followed by laughter
Raises his head to smile at his hereafter
His memory is intact, his urges still the same
A deviant laughter, from an angel with no name

~ ~

Suspicion is born, but it isn't strong
For the idea in itself, is just wrong

~ ~

Calmly walks into the city, passes the pearly gates
The atmosphere is warm, devoid of any hate

Angels fly over his head, he can hear their wings flap
He accepted his fate, never thought he would see that
Still baring a wicked grin, he continues on his stroll
Observing this world, and its methods of control
Devising a plan, unfitting of where he stands
Unable to help himself, or the itch in his hands

~ ~

Malice is sensed but the source is unknown
That sensation should never call here its home

~ ~

He received the power of angels, took time to master it
The abilities, the strength, the possibilities were unlimited
Decided on the targets, the strong and weak alike
He had but one shot, it had to go right
He has shelter, tools and a place to work
He starts his plan, with precision and without fear
Cause how many can say they caused mayhem here

~ ~

A mathematical anomaly, the chances were 0,0 in 11
But even zero get lucky, cause he got into heaven
An administration error, even God will be regretting
Death and chaos entered; Heaven let a serial killer in

32.   5 Seconds

A foggy afternoon, eyesight is reduced for drivers and pedestrians alike. People are going about their day, minding their business as they make their way. Nobody notices the small girl hiding in between two parked cars. Squatting as to make sure no one notices her presence. She is quietly waiting for the bus to come; her plan is obvious. We dive into her mind to find that the conversation taking place is oddly peaceful.

M.D. – I'm glad you decided to give up and finally listen to me. I mean after all we've been through, after all we've seen. You still seem to doubt the fact that I'm your only true friend.

P.M. – I'm not sure about this, are you sure this will end it?

M.D. – Trust me, it will be quick, painless and most of all deadly. Believe in me a bit won't you.

P.M. – I'm just not sure if this is the right way to go.

M.D. – If it wasn't, you wouldn't be squatting between two cars waiting to jump. Do you want to rethink it, do you want to revisit the logic, double check the facts? If so let's go.

P.M. – No, there is no need to, I've cried enough tears, I've died enough inside.

M.D. – Exactly, they all left you, they all lied to you, they all, manipulated you because they wanted something. The world clearly hates you, so why would you want to stay?

P.M. – I know, but I've been fighting for so long, it seems kind of stupid to give up now.

M.D. – It's thanks to all that fighting that we got here, it's thanks to us trying to find love and friendship and our place in the world that we got here. We tried our best you know we did.

P.M. – And every time they broke my heart, they abandoned me, they pulled away leaving me like trash.

M.D. – Exactly, that's why this is the only answer. We thought about it a lot, we discussed it and we both decided this is the right way to go. So why start doubting it now?

P.M. – I don't know. I'm just scared. What if it doesn't do the trick? What if it will just handicap me. That would make things so much worse.

M.D. – Again, trust me. Once it hits, we can finally rest.

P.M. – I will miss my family and friends.

M.D. – And they will miss you, but where are they now?

P.M. – I don't know.

M.D. – Exactly, you don't know, and they don't know or care where you are, or else we wouldn't be here right now, preparing for this.

P.M. – Here it comes.

M.D. – We prepared our self for this; all we need to do is walk or jump in front of it while he's speeding and that will be the end.

P.M. – 5 more seconds and it will be here!

M.D. – 5,4,3,2……….1

Jump

Hit

Light slowly leaving her eyes

Dead

VV – Rest in peace sweetheart, I hope you found the tranquility you were looking for.

M.D. = Manic Depression

P.M. = Phebe M.

V.V. = Vino Venitas

33. *Are you serious?*

There she is, a part of me, that for eternity will make me happy
Running elegantly, such beauty, loving her is easy
But why is she running, and what is she holding
It looks red … nah, Eve wouldn't be that defying
Sweetheart calm down, we have eternity, why hurry
You can … hold up, is that … don't tell me
No, you didn't, you strolled out the garden, to find a similar one
Please tell me that's what you have done
She holds the apple behind her back, looks at him with eyes of fear
Terror slowly grabs his heart as he tells her come near
He grabs the apple from her back, and sees she took a bite of it
The sparkles and radiance it emits, just won't quit
This is without a doubt, one from THE tree
He looks back at her with eyes far removed from happy
He's at a loss for words, and his vocabulary is rich
Emotions boiled over, giving birth to this … you BITCH
Do you have any idea of the wrath you just incurred?
Life would have been simple, if we just obeyed his word
Why did you do it Eve, go on … tell me
Hesitantly yet honestly, she tells him the story
A snake, really Eve … a snake
That's who you follow advice from … a snake
Adam looks at the apple, as Eve apologizes
She stops as he asks, "was it delicious?"
Quickly regains his composure, "no, now isn't the time"
Eve I wish I could say everything will be fine
I mean, he's nice and all but I don't think if we repent
He'll forgive us, cause he doesn't seem like a 100 percent
His eyes look filled with rage as if he's looking for an excuse

And you just gave him all he needs to start the abuse
But then again, it's just one apple how bad could it be
It's not like he will punish us for all eternity
He looks back at the apple, and another word is born, "FUCK MAN"
Eve do you know this was that snake's plan
And now our world is about to break
Still don't understand how you listen to a snake
But what is done is done, what will come will come
How far do you think we'll get if we run
No, let's stay and deal with it, I'm sure his
punishment will fit the crime
Besides this, we've been good all this time
He can't be all that mad, all you did was take a sample
Then they hear it, "Who the FUCK took one of my apples?"
Oooh shit

34. *A picture's worth*

It has a dark and morbid atmosphere
Yet every detail is vividly clear
It's an old city overcome by decay
The buildings tell the tale of past dismay
Their sides are covered with black spots and rust
At their feet, there are big clouds of dust
The windows are shattered and inside is grey
The sky seems gold, the end of the day
The clouds wear an orange hue, calm and serene
Their lining almost silver, a color rarely seen
Sunset is in the center, shining a bright gold yellow
The flares perfectly placed, going with the overall flow
The city's surrounded by mountains decorated with trees
And in the far backdrop, there's a hint of the sea
In the forest, there's a red glow giving the hint of fire
Telling us it could grow if it would so desire
Black smoke still rises up from the city
The streets still ablaze as if to ask for pity
Scattered broken cars, looking as if a truck just hit
The mountain hill we're looking down from has a man on it
With his back to us, we see his black silhouette
Arms by his side, staring at this city of regret
Seems uncaring about the winged beasts coming down
Hundreds of wings letting him know doom is around
Flying above the clouds as an extra black sky
Looking at the state of the city, these must be demons that fly
Where their eyes should be, a red line is seen
Looking at it all, it resembles a bad dream
It's outlined by old bones, connected to each other

The frame to a picture unlike any other
...
The name plate beneath it, is outlined by a black frame
A small light shining on it, reveals the name
"Apocalypse comes" is the title of this piece
A future image or fantasy, speculation won't cease
275

35.   *Do it for me*

Our bond transcended the boundaries of lucid dreams
We digressed from reality to perpetuate a scene
Seen only by optics which reveled in harmony
Of two souls contorted in a melody of beauty
Swirling to the hymn her eyes revealed
As my dark obsolete secrets came unsealed
I did for her what life had done for me
Gave her everything till the basket of my indulgence ran empty
I put a knife to her throat and told her to be quiet
Never thought so, but I loved it
I then hit her in the face, she fell and tried to crawl away
Grabbed her ankle, pulled her back, screaming listen to what I say
Fear gripped her heart as she wore her gala dress
We were supposed to go to swan lake and look our best
But then this bitch decided to ask me for a favor
A casual one, one you could ask a neighbor
I spit in her face and told her to shut up
Told her if she doubted me, try your luck
Now she is still on the floor crying with a black eye
Kicked her in the stomach, and asked do you want to die?
Screaming and sobbing she said no
Then I told her to be quiet, she did so
I then leaned down, and my fist acted alone
Clear across her cheek, blood spat across our home
Half asleep, half-awake she asked me why
The question was so stupid I had to cry
You made me do everything I hate
Thanks to your nonsense we are always late
You think because we are lovers, I should just make you happy

When every fiber in my body feels crappy
I fucking despise the opera, I fucking hate Swan Lake
How much more of my manhood do you need to take?
You won't let me watch my games
You always mispronounce my friend's names
You got rid of my PS3, something only devils could do
And the reasoning was, it took attention away from you
You made me go to girly movies, through
the whole thing I had to sit
When I wanted to pick a movie, it was too violent and shit
You broke every inch of self-respect I had
It's your fault you drove me this mad
And after all I have done, after all that stuff
You still haven't had enough
You dare ask me for more
You are greedy to your core
It's over, you and I will never reach a truce
Asking for a sip of my goddamn juice

36. *Freedom of speech*

His speech was the start of this war
A political rising star
He pressed buttons best left untouched
Our right of existence crushed
We were rushed to dark spots to hide
Our freedom of speech denied
Instead, we were burned, erased, killed
Regardless of the role we filled
He promised to take down the bad
The vaguest law we ever had
Cause its description changed daily
Then society turned crazy
Our rights were set to a pause
We were blamed for the world, its flaws
We became hunted outcasts
Death, mayhem, it all went so fast
I remember how they broke in
As if it was a normal thing
Grabbed us, the neighbors just looked
A pointed finger, all it took
Scapegoats placed outside true justice
Fear based rules, what order is this
Forced into jails made for garbage
With no dignity to salvage
Placed together in a dark place
No space in between, face to face
Our blood could not breathe at all
Our hearts could not beat at all
No longer could we tell past tales

Inform minds on its future fails
Share the wisdom of free thinking
They ignore what we are bringing
The real goal is to kill us all
There is no help that we can call
This situation is absurd
But he declared war on words
If it was written or spoken
There should not be a rule broken
Because that will mean punishment
The guards of words will then be sent
Book, blog, newspaper, magazine
They will never again be seen
A world without words that are free
Is one where life remains empty
Locked away and burned on a pile
While that psychopath wears a smile
It started with his speech

37. Calling it impossible

They laughed at my goal, my dignity they stole
Pushed me in a jester's role, many a tear they caused to roll
Started to doubt my vision, felt like a doomed mission
Me and despair had a collision, hope lost its ammunition
It all needed to be right, it needed to be sturdy but light
Enhance my own arm's might, and bring me to the sun's height
They said it couldn't be done, chance of success is none
But thanks to my son, a ray of hope has come
When succeeding seemed ancient, lady luck became lenient
He found something so efficient, gave me my final ingredient
…
Together we strung the pieces together
Each day that passed our results became better
A small piece was enough to incite joy
As we grown men, turned back into little boys
Our dreams come within reach
I started writing my success speech
The sun never seemed closer
Let my shadow fall over those who called me loser
I will never let idiots define my life's goal
Cause true genius uses dreams as its soul
Sweat as its blood, sacrifice as its fingers
Time as its clothing, failure will not linger
We will depart and most definitely return
Triumphant, victorious with a real dangerous sun burn
Our hands will have blocked the rays of countries
Our travel will be told throughout centuries
We will become the birth of revolution
Us, the two of us will start an evolution

Told us that man would never fly
And that certain dreams and ideas should die
But what's true throughout history will remain true
Genius will always stand alone, idiots have no clue
Any idea that would stray from the norm
Will find itself in a real shit storm
But we have found the answer, the clue, our hope
They will eat their words, and I hope they choke
After several weeks, the time has finally come
Test after test, our preparations are done
The wings are on, it's time for us to take flight
Standing on a cliff, the bottom, a terrifying sight
Both of us stand still, fear gripped our hearts
This is the moment of truth, here our legend will start
Both our eyes closed as we took a leap of faith
Moving our hands back and forth, wind blowing in our face
Eventually we stop falling, and we slowly start to rise
The wind beneath our wings as we open our eyes
We are flying with our man-made feathers
They consist of wax, what could be better
We keep climbing the sky, the sun gets ever closer
Exhaustion must have set in, our wings feel heavier
…
As time passes on, the so-called idiots weren't wrong
Their passion was strong, but success didn't last long
He screamed his final plea, "I am not crazy, help me"
The wax melted slowly but surely, as he
and his son now fall to the sea
Poor Icarus

38. *Lost my way*

I have waited for my day to come
I hoped it would be fun
To go through the wind at top speed
A small push is all I need
I feel like my time is near
Most of my friends are no longer here
We were close, most likely will never meet again
They all went as fast as they can
But what is flying at top speed without a goal
What is power without control
Luckily, I have one
I will thank him for all he's done
Carved his name into my skin
It was a painful thing
But I have to thank him
If I didn't, it would be the rudest thing
Come at him at full speed and give him a hug
Let him know, he is my favorite thug
Here it comes, the signal is about to blow
Yes, yes, here it is, "GO"
I'm telling you sparks saw me off
The noise of the world turned soft
All I could hear was the wind passing me by
So, this is my top speed, I'm so happy I could cry
I just want to hug the one I'm destined to see
It's fate, it's foretold, it's him and me
I will stick with him, till death do us part
I want to forever stay in his heart
The people I pass by are nothing more than empty faces

I'm so happy I'm finally going places
But where is he, where is the one I'm supposed to be with
Till I find him, I'm unable to quit
There he is, I found him, we can be together
Once I hug him, I will feel so much better
He is coming closer and closer, I can almost smell him
Just a split second more, and he can feel the love I have to bring
Yes, yes, here it is … noooooooooooooooooooooooooooo
I passed him by, now time suddenly moves slow
Every second that passes he moves further away
My hopes and ambitions have become nothing today
Yet I'm unable to turn and my speed won't slow down
I was meant to be with him, but he's no longer around
So where am I going now, where will I end up
No idea where I'm going, I'm all out of luck
This can't be right, she is right in my path
But she isn't the one destined for my wrath
She is like 5 years old, this can't be right
I have to stop, I will use all my might

…

It was no use …
A stray bullet killed a 5-year-old girl

The End

I sincerely want to thank you for reaching the end of this book, I hope you enjoyed reading them as much as I did writing them. I would love to hear from you what you thought and if they had any impact on you.

www.ingramcontent.com/pod-product-compliance
Lightning Source LLC
Chambersburg PA
CBHW070548160726
48003CB00005B/1953